CAPTAIN GAMMA

mission to Mars

Written by

Alec Sillifant

Illustrated by

Uwe Meyer

little bee

Captain Gamma was still a little shocked, he hadn't expected to find any life on the planet but at least the alien looked friendly enough.

"I am Captain Gamma," said the spaceman, pointing to the name tag on his spacesuit.

"Want to play hide-and-seek?" asked Flerg excitedly.

And before Captain Gamma could answer, the alien added, **"Great!** You turn around, and I'll go and hide."

And with that the alien ran off.

Captain Gamma turned around,
   closed his eyes and began to count.

1, 2, 3, 4, 5, 6, 7...

The spaceman was brought
out of his daydream
as Flerg shouted,

"Ready!"

from his hiding place.

Captain Gamma opened his eyes and studied the landscape. Most of the planet was flat and covered with little rocks as far as the eye could see, but a little way off was a crater.

Sticking out from behind the crater was a blue bottom.

"Gotcha," thought Captain Gamma,

reaching for his rocket-powered net-gun.

"Coming! Ready or not!"

shouted the spaceman with a wicked grin.

Captain Gamma crept up to the side
of the crater, then, quick as a flash,
jumped behind it and fired his
rocket-powered net-gun...

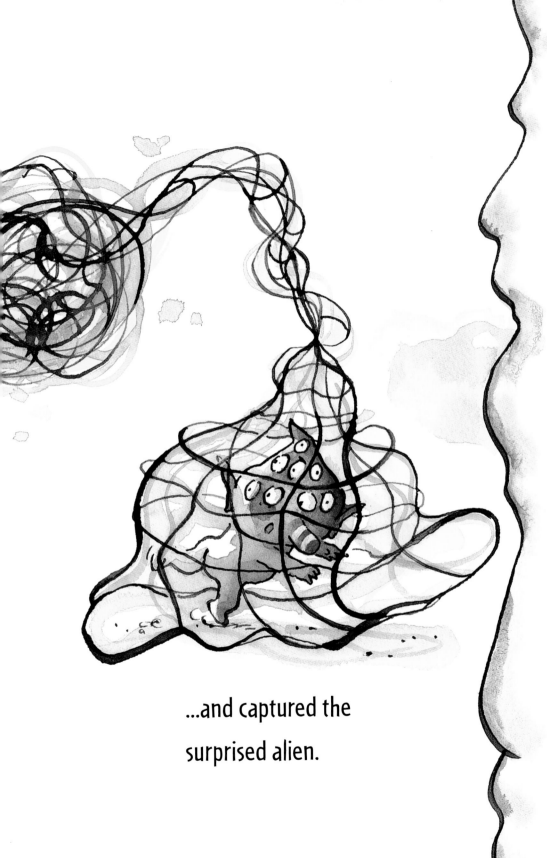

...and captured the
surprised alien.

Flerg smiled. "You're good
at this," he said. "Now it's
my turn to find you."

Captain Gamma was putting
his rocket-powered net-gun
back in its holster.
"No more games
for now Flerg,"
he said. "You're coming
with me."

Captain Gamma began to drag Flerg towards his spaceship.

"Where are we going?" asked the alien.

"Back to Earth," replied Captain Gamma.

"Why?" asked Flerg. "Are we going to play hide-and-seek there?"

"No," snapped the spaceman who was getting very tired.
"You, my blue friend, are going to make me the richest man alive."

Flerg blinked all of his eyes in confusion.
"How can I make you rich by playing hide-and-seek?"

"For the last time," shouted Captain Gamma,
"We aren't going to play hide-and-seek.
I'll probably put you in a cage or
something and then charge
people money to look at the
great big alien
from Mars."

Flerg let out a **really** loud laugh.

"What are you laughing at?" asked Captain Gamma.
"You should have said you wanted
  a great big alien," smiled Flerg.
"What do you mean?"
  asked the spaceman a little puzzled.
"I'm not a great big alien,"
  explained Flerg. Then he
  pointed to something
  behind Captain Gamma.

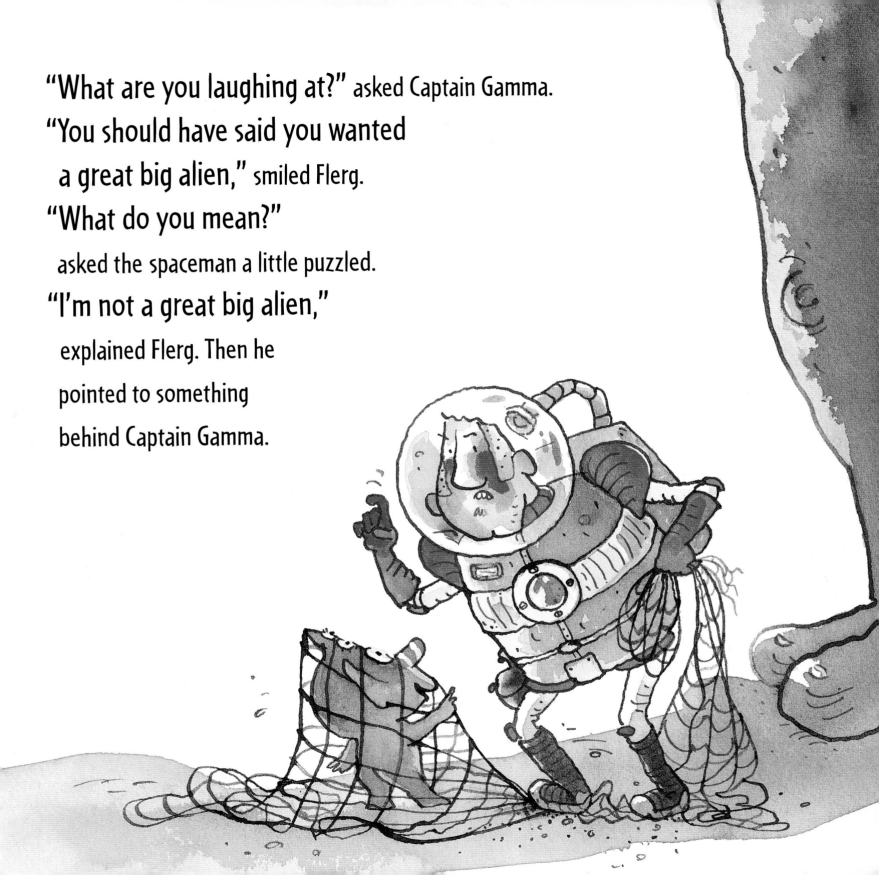

"That's a great big alien."

Quick as a flash Captain Gamma
reached down for his rocket-
powered net-gun again...

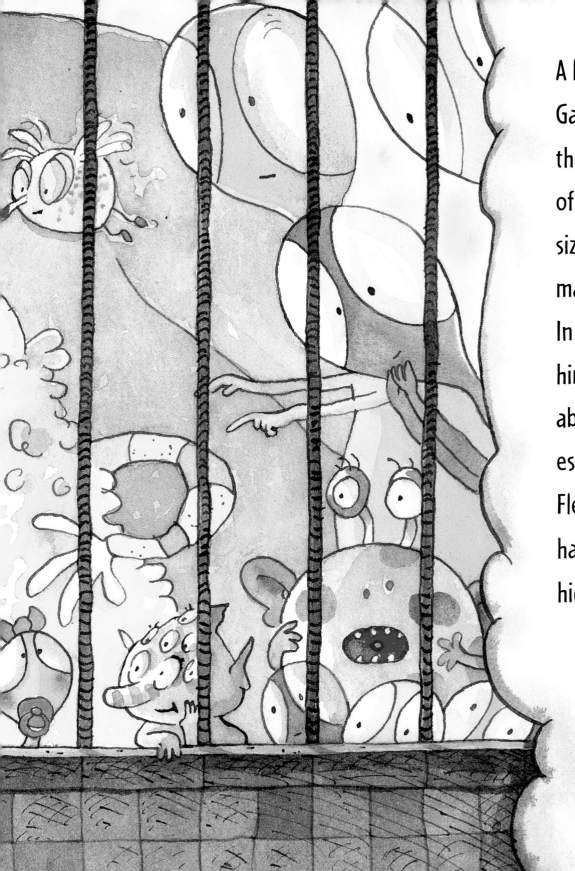

A long time later, Captain Gamma was looking through the bars of a cage at Martians of various shapes, colours and sizes. It was not a sight that made him happy or proud. In fact if he was honest with himself, he had a lot of regrets about his trip to Mars and especially about capturing Flerg, the friendly alien who had only wanted to play hide-and-seek.

Still...

...he'd have plenty of time to think it over while he was the 'Star Attraction' at the

Martian City Zoo.

For Thomas,
welcome to the madness.
A.S.

For Martín, Reuben, Quentin,
and all the other little aliens of this universe.
With lots of love.
U.M.

First published in 2006 by Meadowside Children's Books
185 Fleet Street, London, EC4A 2HS
This edition published in 2007 by Little Bee,
an imprint of Meadowside Children's Books

Text © Alec Sillifant 2006
Illustrations © Uwe Mayer 2006
The rights of Alec Sillifant and Uwe Mayer to be identified as
the author and illustrator of this work have been
asserted by them in accordance with the
Copyright, Designs and Patents Act, 1988

A CIP catalogue record for this book is
available from the British Library
Printed in Indonesia

10 9 8 7 6 5 4 3 2